The Mozart Question

Michael Morpurgo

illustrated by

Michael Foreman

CANDLEWICK PRESS
CAMBRIDGE, MASSACHUSETTS

For Christine Baker—M. M. & M. F.

The question I am most often asked is always easy enough to answer. Question: How did you get started as a writer? Answer: Strangely enough, by asking someone almost exactly that very same question, which I was only able to ask in the first place by receiving a dose of extraordinarily good fortune.

I had better explain.

My good fortune was, of course, someone else's rotten luck—it is often that way, I find. The phone call sounded distraught. It came on a Sunday evening. I had only been working at the paper for three weeks. I was a cub reporter; this, my first paid job.

"Lesley?" It was my boss, chief arts correspondent Meryl Monkton, a lady not to be messed with. She did not waste time with niceties; she never did. "Listen, Lesley, I have a problem. I was due to go to Venice tomorrow to interview Paolo Levi."

"Paolo Levi?" I asked. "The violinist?"

"Is there any other Paolo Levi?" She did not try to hide her irritation. "Now, look, Lesley. I've had an accident, a skiing accident, and I'm stuck in a hospital in Switzerland. You'll have to go to Venice instead of me."

"Oh, that's terrible," I said, smothering as best I could the excitement surging inside me. Three weeks into the job, and I'd be interviewing the great Paolo Levi, and in Venice!

Talk about her accident, I told myself. *Sound concerned. Sound very concerned.*

"How did it happen?" I asked. "The skiing accident, I mean."

"Skiing," she snapped. "If there's one thing I can't abide, Lesley, it's people feeling sorry for me."

"Sorry," I said.

"I would postpone it if I could, Lesley," she went on, "but I just don't dare. It's taken me more than a year to persuade him to do it. It'll be his first interview in years. And even then I had to agree not to ask him the Mozart question. So don't ask him the Mozart question, is that clear? If you do, he'll likely cancel the whole interview—he's done it before. We're really lucky to get him, Lesley. I only wish I could be there to do it myself. But you'll have to do."

"The Mozart question?" I asked rather tentatively.

The silence at the end of the phone was long.

"You mean to say you don't know about Paolo Levi and the Mozart question? Where have you been, girl? Don't you know anything at all about Paolo Levi?"

I suddenly felt I might lose the opportunity altogether if I did not immediately sound informed, and well informed, too.

"Well, he would have been born sometime in the mid-1950s," I began. "He must be about fifty by now."

"Exactly fifty in two weeks' time," Meryl Monkton interrupted wearily. "His London concert is his fiftieth birthday concert. That's the whole point of the interview. Go on."

I rattled off all I knew. "Child prodigy and genius, like Yehudi Menuhin. Played his first major concert when he was thirteen. Probably best known for his playing of Bach and Vivaldi. Like Menuhin, he played often with Grappelli, equally at home with jazz or Scottish fiddle music or Beethoven. Has played in practically every major concert hall in the world, in front of presidents and kings and queens. I heard him at the Royal Festival Hall in London, five years ago, I think. He was playing Beethoven's Violin Concerto; he was wonderful. Doesn't like applause. Never waits for

applause. Doesn't believe in it, apparently. The night I saw him, he just walked off the stage and didn't come back. He thinks it's the music that should be applauded, if anything, or perhaps the composer, but certainly not the musician. Says that the silence after the performance is part of the music and should not be interrupted. Doesn't record, either.

Believes music should be live, not canned. Protects his privacy fiercely. Solitary. Reticent. Lives alone in Venice, where he was born. Just about the most famous musician on the planet, and—"

"*The* most famous, Lesley, but he hates obsequiousness. He likes to be talked to straight. So no bowing or scraping, no wide-eyed wonder, and above all, no nerves. Can you do that?"

"Yes, Meryl," I replied, knowing only too well that I would have the greatest difficulty even finding my voice in front of the great man.

"And whatever you do, stick to the music. He'll talk till the cows come home about music and composers. But no personal stuff. And at all costs, keep off the Mozart question. Oh, yes, and don't take a tape recorder with you. He hates gadgets. Only shorthand. You *can* do shorthand, I suppose? Three thousand words. It's your big chance, so don't mess it up, Lesley."

No pressure, then, I thought.

So there I was the next evening outside Paolo Levi's apartment in the Dorsoduro in Venice, on the dot of six o'clock, my throat dry, my heart pounding, trying to compose myself. It occurred to me again, as it had often on the plane, that I still had no idea what this Mozart question was, only that I mustn't ask it. The night air was cold, the kind of cruel chill that seeps instantly into your bones, deep into your kidneys, and makes your ears ache. This didn't seem to bother the street performers in the square behind me: several grotesquely masked figures on stilts strutting across the square, and an entirely silver statue-man posing immobile outside the café with a gaggle of tourists gazing wonderingly at him.

The door opened, and there he was in front of me, Paolo Levi, neat, trim, his famous hair long to his shoulders and jet black.

"I'm Lesley McInley," I said. "I've come from London."

"From the newspaper, I suppose." There was no welcoming smile. "You'd better come in. Shut the door behind you; I hate the cold." His English was perfect, not a trace of an accent. He seemed to be able to follow my thoughts. "I speak English quite well," he said as we went up the stairs. "Language is like music. You learn it best through listening."

He led me down a hallway and into a large room, empty except for a couch by the window piled high with cushions at one end, a grand piano in the center, and a music stand nearby. At the other end were just two armchairs and a table. Nothing else. "I like to keep it empty," he said.

It was uncanny. He *was* reading my thoughts. Now I felt even more unnerved.

"Sound needs space to breathe, just the same as we need air," he said.

He waved me to a chair and sat down. "You'll have some mint tea?" he said, pouring me a cup. His dark blue cardigan

and gray corduroy trousers were somehow both shabby and elegant at the same time. The bedroom slippers he wore looked incongruous but comfortable. "My feet, they hate the cold more than the rest of me." He was scrutinizing me now,

his eyes sharp and shining. "You're younger than I expected," he said. "Twenty-three?" He didn't wait to have his estimate confirmed—he knew he was right, and he was. "You have heard me play?"

"Beethoven's Violin Concerto. The Royal Festival Hall in London, a few years ago. I was a student." I noticed his violin then, and his bow, on the window ledge.

"I like to practice by the window," he said, "so I can watch the world go by on the canal. It passes the time. Even as a child, I never liked practicing much. And I love to be near water, to look out on it. When I go to London, I have to have a room by the Thames. In Paris I must be by the Seine. I love the light that water makes." He sipped his mint tea, his eyes never leaving me. "Shouldn't you be asking me questions?" He went on. "I'm talking too much. Journalists always make me nervous. I talk too much when I'm nervous. When I go to the dentist's, I talk. Before a concert I talk. So let's get this over with, shall we? And not too many questions, please. Why don't we keep it simple? You ask me one question and then let me ramble on. Shall we try that?" I didn't feel at all that he was being dismissive or patronizing, just straight. That didn't make it any easier, though.

I had done my research, made pages of notes, prepared dozens of questions; but now, under his expectant gaze, I simply could not gather my thoughts.

"Well, I know I can't ask you the Mozart question, Signor Levi," I began, "because I've been told not to. I don't even know what the Mozart question is, so I couldn't ask it even if I wanted to, and anyway, I know you don't like it, so I won't."

With every blundering word, I was digging myself into a deeper hole. In my desperation, I blurted out the first question that came into my head.

"Signor Levi," I said, "I wonder if you'd mind telling me how you got started. I mean, what made you pick up a violin and play that first time?" It was such an obvious question, and personal too, just the kind of question I shouldn't have asked.

His reaction only confirmed that. He sat back in his chair and closed his eyes. For fully a couple of minutes, he said nothing. I was quite sure he was trying to control his impatience, his rage even, that he was going to open his eyes and ask me to leave at once. When he did open his eyes, he simply stared up at the ceiling for a while. I could see from the seriousness of his whole demeanor that he was making a decision, and I feared the worst. But instead of throwing me out, he stood up and walked slowly to the couch by the window. He picked up his violin and sat back on the cushions with his violin resting on his drawn-up knees. He plucked a string or two and tuned it.

"I will tell you a story," he began. "After it is over, you will need to ask me no more questions. Someone once told me that all secrets are lies. The time has come, I think, not to lie anymore."

He paused. I felt he was stiffening his resolve, gathering his strength.

"I will start with my father. Papa was a barber. He kept a little barbershop just behind the Accademia, near the bridge, two minutes from here. We lived above the shop, Mama, Papa, and I, but I spent most of my time downstairs in the barbershop, sitting on the chairs and swinging my legs, smiling at him and his customers in the mirror, and just watching him. I loved those days. I loved him. At the time of these memories, I must have been about nine years old. Small for my age. I always was. I still am."

He spoke slowly, very deliberately, as if he were living it again, seeing again everything he was telling me. My shorthand was quick and automatic, so I had time to look up at him occasionally as he spoke. I sensed right away that I was the first person ever to hear this story, so I knew even as he told it just how momentous the telling of it was for him, and in a totally different way it was for me, too.

"Papa was infinitely deft with his fingers, his scissors playing a constantly changing tune. It seemed to me like a new improvisation for every customer, the snipping unhesitatingly skillful, so fast that it was mesmerizing. He would work always in complete silence, conducting the music of his scissors with his comb. His customers knew better than to interrupt the performance, and so did I. I think perhaps I must have known his customers almost as well as he did. I grew up with them. They were all regulars. Some would close their eyes as Papa worked his magic; others would look back in the mirror at me and wink.

"Shaving was just as fascinating to me, just as rhythmical too: the swift sweep and dab of the brush, the swish and slap of the razor as Papa sharpened it on the strap, then each time the miraculous unmasking as he stroked the foam away to reveal a recognizable face once more.

"After it was all over, he and his customers did talk, and all the banter among them was about soccer, Inter Milan in particular, or sometimes the machinations of politicians and women. What they said I cannot exactly remember, probably because I couldn't understand most of it, but I do know they

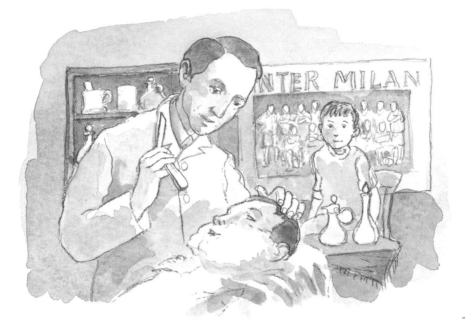

laughed a lot. I do remember that. Then the next customer would take his seat, and a new silence would descend before the performance started again and the music of the scissors began. I am sure I first learned about rhythm in that barbershop, and about concentration. I learned to listen, too.

"Papa wasn't just the best barber in all of Venice—everyone said that—he was a musician too, a violinist. But strangely he was a violinist who never played the violin. I never heard him play, not once. I only knew he was a violinist because Mama had told me so. She had tears in her eyes whenever she told me about it. That surprised me, because she was not a crying woman. He had been so brilliant as a violinist, the best in the whole orchestra, she said. When I asked why he didn't play anymore, she turned away from me, went very quiet, and told me I'd have to ask Papa myself. So I did. I asked him time and again, and each time he would simply shrug and say something meaningless like: 'People change, Paolo. Times change.' And that would be that.

"Papa was never a great talker at the best of times, even at home, but I could tell that in this case he was hiding something, that he found my questions both irksome and intrusive. That didn't stop me. I kept at him. Every time he refused to talk about it, I became more suspicious, more sure he had something to hide. It was a child's intuition, I suppose. I sensed a deep secret, but I also sensed after a while that Papa was quite unmovable, that if I were ever going to unlock the secret, it would be Mama who would tell me.

"As it turned out, my instinct was right. In the end, my almost perpetual pestering proved fruitful, and Mama capitulated—but not in a way I had expected. 'All right, Paolo,' she said after I'd been nagging her about it unmercifully one morning. 'If I show you the violin, will you promise me you'll stop asking your wretched questions? And you're never, ever to tell Papa I showed you. He'd be very angry. Promise me now.'

"So I promised, promised faithfully, and then stood in their bedroom and watched as she climbed up on a chair to get it down from where it had been hidden on top of the cupboard. It was wrapped up in an old gray blanket. I knelt on the bed beside her as she pulled away the blanket and opened the violin case. I remember it smelled musty. The maroon lining inside was faded and worn to tatters. Mama picked up the violin with infinite care, reverently almost. Then she handed it to me.

"I stroked the polished grain of the wood, which was the color of honey, dark honey on the front, and golden honey underneath. I ran my fingers along the black pegs, the mottled bridge, the exquisitely carved scroll. It was so light to hold, I remember. I wondered at its fragile beauty. I knew at once that all the music in the world was hidden away inside this violin, yearning to come out. I longed to be the one to let it out, to rest it under my chin, to play the strings, to try the bow. I wanted there and then to bring it to life, to have it sing for me, to hear all the music we could make together. But when I asked if I could play it, Mama took a sudden fright and said Papa might hear down below in the barbershop and be furious with her for showing it to me, that he never wanted it to be played again. He hadn't so much as looked at it in years. When I asked why, she reminded me of my promise not to ask any more questions. She almost snatched the violin away from me, laid it back in its case, wrapped it again in the blanket, and put it back up on top of the cupboard.

"'You don't know it exists, Paolo. You never saw it, understand? And from now on I don't want to hear another word about it, all right? You promised me, Paolo.'

"I suppose seeing Papa's old violin, holding it as I had, marveling at it must have satisfied my curiosity for a while, because I kept my promise. Then late one summer's evening, I was lying half awake in my bed when I heard the sound of a violin. I thought Papa must have changed his mind and was playing again at last. But then I heard him and Mama talking in the kitchen below and realized that the music was coming from much farther away.

"I listened at the window. I could hear it only intermittently over the sound of people talking and walking, over the throbbing engines of passing water taxis, but I was quite sure now that it was coming from somewhere beyond the bridge. I had to find out. In my pajamas I stole past the kitchen door, down the stairs, and out into the street. It was a warm night and quite dark. I ran up over the bridge, and there, all on his own, standing by the lamp in the square, was an old man playing the violin, his violin case open at his feet.

"No one else was there. No one had stopped to listen. I squatted down as close as I dared. He was so wrapped up in his playing that he did not notice me at first. I could see now that he was much older than Papa. Then he saw me crouching there, watching him. He stopped playing. 'Hello,' he said. 'You're out late. What's your name?' He had kind eyes; I noticed that at once.

"'Paolo,' I told him. 'Paolo Levi. My papa plays the violin. He played in an orchestra once.'

"'So did I,' said the old man, 'all my life. But now I am what I always wanted to be, a soloist. I shall play you some Mozart. Do you like Mozart?'

"'I don't know,' I replied. I knew Mozart's name, of course, but I don't think I had ever listened to any of his music.

"'He wrote this piece when he was even younger than you. I should guess that you're about seven.'

"'Nine,' I said.

"'Well, Mozart wrote this when he was just six years old. He wrote it for the piano, but I can play it on the violin.'

"So he played Mozart, and I listened. As he played, others

came and gathered around for a while before dropping a coin or two in his violin case and moving on. I didn't move on. I stayed. The music he played to me that night touched my soul. It was the night that changed my life forever.

"Whenever I crossed the Accademia Bridge after that, I always looked for him. Whenever I heard him playing, I went to listen. I never told Mama or Papa. I think it was the first secret I kept from them. But I did not feel guilty about it, not one bit. After all, hadn't they kept a secret from me? Then one evening the old man—I had found out by now that his name was Benjamin Horowitz and that he was sixty-two years old—one evening he let me hold his violin, showing me how to hold it properly, how to draw the bow across the strings, how to make it sing. The moment I did that, I knew I had to be a violinist. I have never wanted to do or be anything else since.

"So Benjamin—Signor Horowitz, I always called him then—became my first teacher. Now every time I ran over the bridge to see him, he would show me a little more, how to tighten the bow just right, how to use the resin, how to hold the violin under my chin using no hands at all, and what each string was called. That was when I told him about Papa's violin at home and about how he didn't play it anymore. 'He couldn't anyway,' I said, 'because it's a bit broken. I think it needs mending. Two of the strings are missing, the A and the E, and there's hardly a hair left on the bow at all. But I could practice on it if it was mended, couldn't I?'

"'Bring it to my house sometime,' Benjamin said, 'and leave it with me. I'll see what I can do.'

"It wasn't difficult to escape unnoticed. I just waited until after school. Mama was still at the laundry around the corner in Rio de le Romite, where she worked. Papa was downstairs with his customers. To reach the violin on top of the cupboard, I had to put a suitcase on the chair and then climb up. It

wasn't easy, but I managed. I ran through the streets hugging it to me. From the Dorsoduro to the Arsenale, where Benjamin lived, is not that far if you know the way—nowhere is that far in Venice—and I knew the way quite well, because my aunt Sophia lived there and we visited her often. All I had to do was find Benjamin's street. I had to ask for help, but I found it.

"Benjamin lived up a narrow flight of stairs in one small room with a bed in one corner and a basin in the other. On the wall were lots of concert posters. 'Some of the concerts I played,' he said. 'Milan, London, New York. Wonderful places, wonderful people, wonderful music. It is a wonderful world out there. There are times when it can be hard to go on believing that. But always believe it, Paolo, because it is true. And music helps to make it so. Now, show me that violin of yours.'

"He studied it closely, holding it up to the light, tapping it. 'A very fine instrument,' he said. 'You say this belongs to your father?'

"'And now I want to play it myself,' I told him.

"'It's a bit on the large side for a young lad like you,' he said, tucking the violin under my chin and stretching my arm to see how far I could reach. 'But a big violin is better than no violin at all. You'll manage. You'll grow into it.'

"'And when it's mended, will you teach me?' I asked him. 'I've got lots of money saved up from my sweeping; so many *lire* they cover all my bed when I spread them out, from the end of the bed right up to my pillow.'

"He laughed at that and told me he would teach me for nothing because I was his best listener, his lucky mascot. 'When you're not there,' he said, 'everyone walks by, and my violin case stays empty. Then you come along and sit there.

That's when they always stop to listen, and that's when they leave their money. So a lesson or two will just be paying you back, Paolo. I'll have the violin ready as soon as I can, and then we can start your lessons.'

"It was a week or two before the violin was mended. I dreaded that Mama or Papa might discover it was missing. But my luck held, and they didn't, and

my lessons began. Whenever I wasn't having my lessons with Benjamin, Papa's violin, now restrung and restored, lay in its case wrapped in the gray blanket and hidden away on top of their bedroom cupboard. My secret was safe, I thought. But secrets are never safe, however well hidden. Sooner or later the truth will come out, and in this case it was to be sooner rather than later.

"I took to the violin as if it had been a limb I had been missing all my life. I seemed to be able to pick up everything Benjamin taught me, effortlessly and instinctively. Under his kind tutelage, my confidence simply burgeoned, my playing blossomed. I found I could make my violin—Papa's violin, rather—sing with the voice of an angel. Benjamin and I felt the excitement and pleasure of my progress as keenly as each other. 'I think this instrument was invented just for you, Paolo,' he told me one day. 'Or maybe you were made for it. Either way, it is a perfect match.' I loved every precious moment of my lessons and always dreaded their ending. We would finish every lesson with a cup of mint tea made with fresh mint. I loved it. Ever since, I have always treated myself to a cup of mint tea after practice. It's something I always look forward to.

"I remember one day with the lesson over, we were drinking tea at his table when he looked across at me, suddenly very serious. 'It is strange, Paolo,' he said, 'but as I was watching you playing a moment ago, I felt I had known you before, a long, long time ago. And then just now I thought about your name, Levi. It is a common enough name, I know, but

his name was Levi too. It is him you remind me of. I am sure of it. He was the youngest player in our orchestra, no more than a boy, really. Gino, he was called.'

"'But my father is named Gino,' I told him. 'Maybe it was him. Maybe you played with my father. Maybe you know him.'

"'It can't be possible,' Benjamin breathed. He was staring at me now as if I were a ghost. 'No, it can't be. The Gino Levi I knew must be dead, I am sure of it. I have not heard of him in a long while, a very long while. But you never know, I suppose. Maybe I should meet your papa, and your mama too. It's about time, anyway. You've been coming for lessons for over six months now. They need to know they have a wonderful violinist for a son.'

"'No, you can't!' I cried. 'He'd find out! You can't tell him. You mustn't!' Then I told him, through my tears, all about my secret, about how Mama had shown me Papa's violin and made me promise never to say anything, never to tell Papa, and how I'd kept it a secret all this while, mending the violin, the lessons, everything.

"'Secrets, Paolo,' said Benjamin, 'are lies by another name. You do not lie to those you love. A son should not hide things from his papa and his mama. You must tell them your secret, Paolo. If you want to go on playing the violin, you will have to tell them. If you want me to go on teaching you, you will have to tell them. And now is usually a good time to do what must be done, particularly when you don't want to do it.'

"'Will you come with me?' I begged him. 'I can only do it if you come with me.'

"'If you like,' he said, smiling.

"Benjamin carried Papa's violin for me that day and held my hand all the way back to the Dorsoduro. I dreaded having to make my confession. I knew how hurt they would be. All the way I rehearsed what I was going to say over and over again.

Mama and Papa were upstairs in the kitchen when we came in. I introduced Benjamin and then, before anyone had a chance to say anything, before I lost my courage entirely, I launched at once into my prepared confession, how I hadn't really stolen Papa's violin, just borrowed it to get it mended and to practice on. But that's as far as I got. To my surprise, they were not looking angry. In fact, they weren't looking at me at all. They were just staring up at Benjamin as if quite unable to speak. Benjamin spoke before they did. 'Your mama and papa and I, I think perhaps we do know one another,' he said. 'We played together once, did we not? Don't you remember me, Gino?'

"'Benjamin?' As Papa started to his feet, the chair went over behind him.

"'And if I am not much mistaken, Signora,' Benjamin went on, looking now at Mama, 'you must be little Laura Adler—all of us violins, all of us there, and all of us still here. It is like a miracle. It *is* a miracle.'

"What happened next I can see as if it were yesterday. It was suddenly as if I were not in the room at all. The three of them seemed to fill the kitchen, arms around each other,

and crying openly, crying through their laughter. I stood
there mystified, trying to piece together all I had heard, all
that was going on before my eyes. Mama played the violin too!
She had never told me that!

"'You see, Paolo,' said Benjamin, smiling down at me, 'didn't I tell you once it was a wonderful world? Twenty years. It's been twenty years or more since I last saw your mama and papa. I had no idea they were still alive. I always hoped they survived, hoped they were together, these two young love-birds, but I never believed it, not really.'

"Mama was drying her eyes on her apron. Papa was so overcome, he couldn't speak. They sat down then, hands joined around the table as if unwilling to let each other go for fear this reunion might turn out to be no more than a dream.

"Benjamin was the first to recover. 'Paolo was about to tell you something, I think,' he said. 'Weren't you, Paolo?' I told them everything then: how I'd gone for my lessons, how Benjamin had been the best teacher in all the world. I dared to look up only when I'd finished. Instead of the disapproval and disappointment I had expected, both Mama and Papa were simply glowing with joy and pride.

"'Didn't I say Paolo would tell us, Papa?' she said. 'Didn't I tell you we should trust him? You see, Paolo, I often take down my violin, just to touch it, to look at it. Papa doesn't like me to, but I do it all the same, because this violin is my oldest friend. Papa forgives me, because he knows I love this violin, that it is a part of me. You remember I showed it to you that day, Paolo? It wasn't long after that that it went missing, was it? I knew it had to be you. Then it came back, mended miraculously. And after school you were never home, and when you weren't home, the violin was always gone too. I told Papa, didn't I, Papa? I told him you'd tell us when you were ready. We put two and two together; we thought you might be practicing somewhere, but it never occurred to us that you were having lessons, nor that you had a teacher—and certainly not that your teacher was Benjamin Horowitz, who taught us and looked after us like a father all those years ago.' She cried again then, her head on Papa's shoulder.

"'But you told me it was Papa's violin, that he'd put it away and never wanted to play it again, ever,' I said.

"At this, the three of them looked at one another. I knew then that they all shared the same secret, and that without a word passing between them they were deciding whether they should reveal it, if this was the right moment to tell me. I often wondered later whether, if Benjamin had not come that day, they would ever have told me. As it was, they looked to Papa for the final decision, and it was he who invited me to the table to join them. I think I knew then, even before Papa began, that I was in some way part of their secret.

"'Mama and I,' Papa began, 'we try never to speak of this, because the memories we have are like nightmares, and we want to forget. But you told us your secret. There is a time for truth, it seems, and it has come. Truth for truth, maybe.'

"So began the saddest, yet the happiest story I ever heard. When the story became too painful, as it often did, they passed it from one to the other, so that all three shared it. I listened, horrified, and at the same time honored that they trusted me enough with their story, the story of their lives. Each told their part with great care, explaining as they went along so that I would understand, because I was a boy of nine who knew very little then of the wickedness of the world. I wish I could remember their exact words, but I can't, so I won't even try. I'll just tell you their story my own way, about how they lived together, how they nearly died together, and how they were saved by music.

"The three of them were brought by train to the concentration camp from all over Europe: Benjamin from Paris, Mama from Warsaw, Papa from here, from Venice; all musicians, all Jewish, and all bound for the gas chamber and extermination like so many millions. They survived only because they were all able to say yes to one question put to them by an SS officer on arrival at the camp. 'Is there anyone among you who can play an orchestral instrument, who is a professional musician?' They did not know when they stepped forward that they would at once be separated from their families, would have to watch them being herded off toward those hellish chimneys, never to be seen again.

"There were auditions, of course, and by now they knew they were playing for their lives. There were rehearsals then, and it was during these rehearsals that the three of them met. Benjamin was a good twenty years older than Mama and Papa, who were very much the babies of the orchestra, both of them just twenty. Why the orchestra was rehearsing, who they would be playing for, they did not know and they did not ask. To ask was to draw attention to oneself. This they knew was not the way to survive, and in the camp, to survive was everything. They played Mozart, a lot of Mozart. The repertoire was for the most part light and happy—*Eine Kleine Nachtmusick*, the Clarinet Concerto in A Major, minuets, dances, marches. And Strauss was popular too—waltzes, always waltzes. Playing was very hard, because their fingers were so cold that sometimes they could hardly feel them, because they were weak with hunger and frequently sick. Sickness had to be hidden, because sickness, once discovered, would mean death. The SS men were always there watching, and everyone knew too what awaited them if they did not play well enough.

"At first they gave concerts only for the SS officers. Papa said you just had to pretend they were not there. You simply lost yourself in the music—it was the only way. Even when they applauded, you did not look up. You never looked them in the eye. You played with total commitment. Every performance was your best performance, not to please them, but to show them what you could do, to prove to them how good you

were, despite all they were doing to humiliate you, to destroy you in body and soul. 'We fought back with our music,' Papa said. 'It was our only weapon.'

"Papa could speak no Polish, Mama no Italian, but their
eyes met as they were playing—as often as possible, Mama
said. To begin with, it might have been their shared joy
in music-making, but very soon they knew they loved each

other. The whole orchestra knew it, even before they did, Benjamin told me. 'Our little lovebirds' they were called. For everyone else in the orchestra, he said, they represented a symbol of hope for the future; and so they were much loved, much protected. For Mama and Papa, their love numbed the pain and was a blessed refuge from the constant fear they were living through, from the horror of all that was going on around them.

"But there was among them a shared shame. They were being fed when others were not. They were being kept alive while others went to the gas chamber. Many were consumed by guilt, and this guilt was multiplied a thousand times when they discovered the real reason the orchestra had been assembled, why they had been rehearsing all this time. The concerts for the SS officers turned out to be sinister dress rehearsals for something a great deal worse.

"One cold morning with snow on the ground, they were made to assemble out in the compound with their instruments and ordered to sit down and play close to the camp gates. Then the train arrived, the cars packed with new prisoners.

Once they were all out, they were lined up and then divided. The old and young and the frail were herded past the orchestra on their way, they were told, to the shower block; the able-bodied, those fit for work, were taken off toward the huts. And all the while, Mama and Papa and Benjamin and the others played their Mozart. They all understood soon enough what it was for—to calm the terror, to beguile each new trainload into a false sense of security. They were part of a deadly sham. They knew well enough that the shower block was a gas chamber.

"Week after week they played, month after month, train after train. And twenty-four hours a day, the chimneys of the crematorium spewed out their fire and their smoke and their stench. Until there were no more trains, until the day the camps were liberated. This was the last day Benjamin ever remembered seeing Mama and Papa. They were all terribly emaciated by now, he said, and looked unlikely to survive. But they had. Mama and Papa had walked together out of the camp. They had played duets for bread and shelter, all across Europe. They were still playing to survive.

"When at last they got home to Venice, Papa smashed his violin and burned it, vowing never to play music again. But Mama kept hers. She thought of it as her talisman, her savior, and her friend, and she would neither sell it nor abandon it. She said it had brought her through all the hor- rors of the camp, brought them safely across Europe, back to Papa's home in Venice. It had saved their lives.

"Papa kept his vow. He never played a note of music again. After all that had happened, he could hardly bear to hear it, which is why Mama had not played her violin either in all these years. But she would not be parted from it and had kept it safe at the top of their bedroom cupboard, hoping against hope, she said, that one day Papa might change his mind and be able to love music again and even play it. He never had. But they had survived, and they were in time blessed with a child, a boy they called Paolo—a happy ending, Benjamin said. And I was the one who had brought the three of them together again, he said. So two happy endings.

"As for Benjamin, he had found his way back to Paris after a while and played again in his old orchestra. He had married a French woman, Françoise, a cellist who had died only recently. He had come to Venice because he had always loved visiting the city and always longed to live looking out over water, and because Vivaldi was born here—he had always loved Vivaldi above all other composers. He played in the streets not just for the money, though that was a help, but because he could not bear not to play his violin. And he loved playing solo violin at last. He was more like Mama, he said. It was music that had kept him alive in the camp, and music had been his constant companion ever since. He could not imagine living a single day of his life without it, which was

why, he said, he would dearly like to go on teaching me, if Mama and Papa would allow it.

"'Does he play well, Benjamin?' Mama asked. 'Can we hear him, Papa? Please.'

"Papa, I could see, was struggling with himself. 'So long as it's not Mozart,' he said finally. So I played the Winter concerto from Vivaldi's *Four Seasons*, Benjamin's favorite piece. Papa sat listening with closed eyes throughout.

"When I had finished, Benjamin said, 'Well, Gino, what do you think? He has a great and wonderful talent, your son, a rare gift you have both given him.'

"'Then it must not be wasted,' said Papa quietly.

"So every day without fail after that, I went for my violin lessons with Benjamin in his little apartment in the Arsenale. Papa could not bring himself to listen to me playing, but sometimes Mama came along with me and sat and listened, and afterward she always hugged me so tight it hurt, but I did not mind, not one bit. I began to play in the streets alongside Benjamin, and whenever I did, the crowds became bigger and bigger each time. One day Papa was there among them,

watching, listening. He walked me home afterward, saying not a word until we were walking over the Accademia Bridge. 'So, Paolo,' he said, 'you prefer playing the violin to sweeping up in my barbershop, do you?'

"'Yes, Papa,' I replied. 'I'm afraid I do.'

"'Well then, I can see I shall just have to do my sweeping up myself.' He stopped then and put his hands on my shoulders. 'I shall tell you something, Paolo, and I want you never to forget it. When you play, I can listen to music again. You have made music joyful for me once more, and that is a wonderful gift you have given me. You go and be the great violinist you should be. I shall help you all I can. You will play heavenly music, and people will love you. Mama and I shall come to all your concerts, or as many as we can. But you have to promise me one thing: that until the day I die, you will never play Mozart in public, not in my hearing. It was Mozart we played so often in the camp. Never Mozart. Promise me.'

"So I promised. I have kept my promise to Papa all these years. He died two weeks ago, the last of the three of them to go.

At my fiftieth birthday concert in London, I shall be playing Mozart, and I shall be playing it on Mama's violin, and I shall play it so well that he will love it, they will all love it, wherever they are."

I was still finishing my shorthand when I looked up and saw him coming toward me. He was offering me his violin.

"Here you are," he said. "Mama's violin. My violin. You can hold it if you like while we have some more mint tea. You'll have another cup, won't you? I make the best mint tea in Venice."

So I held Paolo Levi's violin for several precious minutes as we sat talking quietly over a last cup of tea. I asked him no more questions. There were none to ask. He talked of his love of Venice, and how wherever he was in the world he longed to be back home. It was the sounds he always missed: the church bells, the walking and talking, the chugging of boats, and the music in the streets. "Music belongs in the streets, where Benjamin played it," he said, "not in concert halls."

As I left, he looked me in the eye and said, still grasping my hand, "I am glad it was you I told."

"Why did you?" I asked. "Why did you tell me?"

"Because it was time to tell the truth. Because secrets are lies, and because you have eyes that are kind, like Benjamin's. But mostly because you didn't ask the Mozart question."

Author's Note

It is difficult for us to imagine how dreadful the suffering was that went on in the Nazi concentration camps during the Second World War. The enormity of the crime that the Nazis committed is too overwhelming for us to comprehend. In their attempt to wipe out an entire race, they caused the deaths of six million people, most of them Jews. It is when we hear the stories of the individuals who lived through it—Anne Frank, Primo Levi—that we can begin to understand the horror just a little better, and to understand the evil that caused it.

For me, the most haunting image does not come from literature or film but from music. I learned some time ago that in many of the camps the Nazis selected Jewish prisoners and forced them to play in orchestras; for the musicians it was simply a way to survive. In order to calm the new arrivals at the camps, the musicians were made to serenade them as they were lined up and marched off, many to the gas chambers. Often they played Mozart.

I wondered how it must have been for a musician who played in such hellish circumstances who adored Mozart as I do—what thoughts came when playing Mozart later in life. This was the genesis of my story—this and the sight of a small boy in a square by the Accademia Bridge in Venice, sitting one night in his pajamas on his tricycle, listening to a street musician. He sat totally enthralled by the music that seemed to him, and to me, to be heavenly.

Michael Morpurgo

This is a work of fiction. Names, characters, places, and incidents are either products of the author's imagination or, if real, are used fictitiously.

Text copyright © 2006 by Michael Morpurgo • Illustrations copyright © 2007 by Michael Foreman

All rights reserved. No part of this book may be reproduced, transmitted, or stored in an information retrieval system in any form or by any means, graphic, electronic, or mechanical, including photocopying, taping, and recording, without prior written permission from the publisher.

First U.S. edition 2008

Library of Congress Cataloging-in-Publication Data is available. Library of Congress Catalog Card Number pending

ISBN 978-0-7636-3552-7

2 4 6 8 10 9 7 5 3 1

Printed in China

This book was typeset in Bodoni. The illustrations were done in pencil and watercolor.

Candlewick Press, 2067 Massachusetts Avenue, Cambridge, Massachusetts 02140

visit us at www.candlewick.com